DIANE Z. SHORE AND JESSICA ALEXANDER

THIS IS THE EARTH

PAINTINGS BY WENDELL MINOR

HARPER
An Imprint of HarperCollinsPublishers

This is the land,
fertile, alive,
crawling with creatures
that help it to thrive.

This is the river,
flowing and free,
streaming with fish
as it swells to the sea.

This is the sky,
endless and blue,
speckled with birds
as they soar into view.

This is the Earth, washed by the rain
that fills up the creek and spills over the plain
and nurtures the soil, planted with seed,
so people can harvest the food that they need

and build houses from stones
and from trees cut by hand
in the towering forests
that shelter the land
that protects and preserves
those who tend it with care
as together we live on this Earth that we share.

This is the spike
driven into the ground
for the railways connecting
the fast-growing towns.

This is the steamer
with coal and with wood
transporting its cargo
of people and goods.

This is the plane
as it roars into flight,
stretching its wings
and reaching new heights.

This is the Earth, where new buildings rise
into towers of steel overshadowing skies
as workers pour roadways of concrete and tar
so commuters can travel by bus and by car
to the cities for jobs that will pay a fair wage
in this fast-moving, busy industrial age
when we build, we expand, we invent, and we dare,
and we change how we live on this Earth that we share.

This is the landfill,
a growing gray mound
of garbage that steams
on the sweltering ground.

This is the pipe
draining into the sea,
spilling out wastewater,
muck, and debris.

This is the smoke
billowing black,
spewing from chimneys
and factory stacks.

This is the Earth, polluted by greed,
as we take what we want, which is more than we need,
where bulldozing trucks clear the rainforest floor
and sands wash away from the vanishing shore,

where huge Arctic glaciers melt into the sea
and fumes and exhaust choke the air that we breathe,
endangering nature, creating despair—
we forget how to live on this Earth that we share.

These are the bins
where the bottles and cans
and the papers await
the recycling vans.

This is the bicycle, racing to school;
the pedaling rider provides all the fuel.
This is the faucet, where every drop counts,
releasing the water in careful amounts.

This is the Earth that we treat with respect,
where people and animals interconnect,
where we learn to find balance between give and take
and help heal the planet with choices we make,

like walking or biking, not taking the car,
or sharing a ride if the journey is far,
using less water to get ourselves clean,
planting trees in the city to help it grow green,

bringing reusable bags to the store,
and flipping the switch when we head out the door.

Making a difference,
becoming aware,
together we live
on this Earth that we share.

A NOTE FROM THE AUTHORS

The Earth is our home. It is where we live, breathe, eat, and play. Just as we have responsibilities at home like cleaning our room and feeding our pets, it is our responsibility to keep our planet healthy.

"Going green" can be easy. Little things like turning off the water when we brush our teeth, carpooling to activities and events, and recycling and reusing materials will help reduce the waste in our landfills, make the air we breathe cleaner, and keep the planet safe for all living things.

For more ideas on how you can make a difference, visit www.earthday.com.

— *Diane Shore and Jessica Alexander*

A NOTE FROM THE ILLUSTRATOR

When Apollo 8 astronaut Bill Anders took his historic photo of the Earth rising over the moon's horizon on Christmas Eve 1968, it was the first time we were able to see how fragile our home planet really is: a tiny bright blue-and-white marble floating in the blackness of never-ending space. As Bill Anders said, "We came all this way to explore the moon, and the most important thing is that we discovered the Earth."

Bill Anders's photo contributed to an awareness of what was a growing concern about the well-being of our planet. April 22, 1970, was the first celebration of Earth Day and the birth of the environmental movement that we know today.

There are little things we can all do every day to help conserve energy, food, and water to live a greener life that will give us a brighter future on the only home we have, planet Earth!

— *Wendell Minor*

Library of Congress Control Number: 2015936056

ISBN 978-0-06-055526-9 (trade bdg.) — ISBN 978-0-06-055527-6 (lib. bdg.)

The artist used Windsor and Newton Watercolors on archival 3-ply Strathmore Bristol paper to create the illustrations for this book.

Typography by Dana Fritts

15 16 17 18 19 SCP 10 9 8 7 6 5 4 3 2 1

❖

First Edition